# Nightlight

Jeannine Anderson

Nikki Johnson

Joy Dey

**Windward** Publishing
AN IMPRINT OF FINNEY COMPANY

# Nightlight

ISBN 0-89317-056-9 hardcover
ISBN 0-89317-057-7 softcover

10 9 8 7 6 5 4 3 2 1

Printed in the United States of America

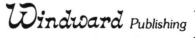

**Windward** Publishing
AN IMPRINT OF FINNEY COMPANY
www.finney-hobar.com

3943 Meadowbrook Road
Minneapolis, MN  55426-4505

# Dedication

For Tom Robbins, my perfect partner in love and life.
For Maynard, Angie, and Connie, my fantastic family.
And for Char, Norma, Karen, and Joanne, four forever friends.
— *Nikki*

To my family, who are fascinated by the northern lights.
— *Jeannine*

For Mark, the forest ranger I met and fell in love with
one magical night aglow with fireflies and northern lights.
— *Joy*

## Special thanks to . . .

Donald McNeely and his family for their inspiring enthusiasm.

Thomas Eugenius Kress for generously sharing his technical expertise.

Al Krysan for having the vision to share our vision.

Karli Anderson for bringing us together to make a book.

Carlene Sippola for examining this book's potential with a publisher's practiced eye.

Susan Gustafson, friend and publishing maven, for bestowing her characteristic gentle, but on-target criticism and clear focus to this project, thank heaven.

Don and Nancy Tubesing for applying their wealth of publishing experience, especially their special genius for seeing "the big picture," to the betterment of this story.

Aurora Mae and Borealis Burl were two very adventurous little bears.

They scurried through the forest chasing one another . . .

Turning over rocks

Sliding down cliffs

Playing hide and seek in the wild flowers

and Cooling off in the river waters.

Around every tree trunk was a new surprise.

Aurora Mae discovered that honey
isn't always easy to get.

Borealis Burl discovered that tree limbs aren't always the best places to nap.

As day gave way to nightfall,
the two little bears found a safe place to sleep
under the vast night sky.

With heavy eyes, they listened
to the calming of the evening.

Nearby, a moose munched in a swamp.
From a tree, an owl hunted.
And frogs croaked in a pond.

nd as the two bears dozed,
the sky began to stir.

With a whisper, the emerald sky rippled.
The moose stopped chewing and looked up.

Gentle waves of green and blue rolled across the sky.
The croaking frogs paused.

**D**elicate, white fingers of light seemed to reach out.
The owl cocked his head toward the light.

**H**igh above, the heavens
continued to move.
Startled, a squirrel stopped
and glanced upward,
accidentally dropping
a nut on the sleeping bears.

They awoke. Huddling close,
the bears peered into the sky.
They could feel the magic of the night.

Wings seemed to appear
and glide across the sky.
Aurora Mae and Borealis Burl
were not afraid.

The bears gazed in wonder.
What could this be?

An arc.

A swirl.

A burst of color.

The sky was ablaze
with a yellow glow.
Burning candles
seemed to fill the night sky.
And the bears' eyes widened.

# Rapidly changing.

Dazzling.
Red and orange swirling,
like a giant brush fire in the sky.

xcitement grew.

Thousands of fireflies began flickering among the trees.

The animals waited breathlessly.

**An explosion!**

The northern lights filled the sky, illuminating the forest.

The bears blinked.
The moose stepped back.
The owl's eyes grew large.
The frogs jumped in surprise.

The forest never looked so radiant.

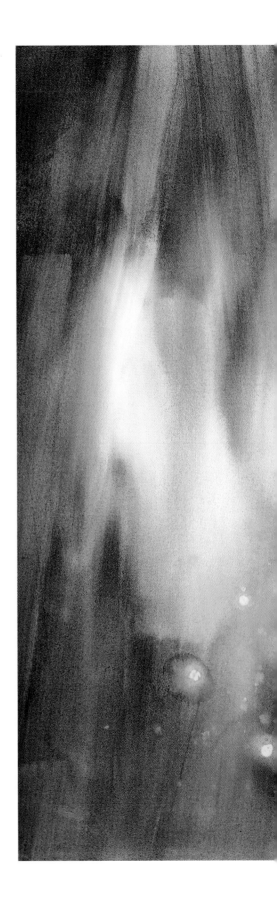

**T**hen, into the magical night,
the bears promenaded through the
forest with fireflies as their guide.

They did not stumble or fall into holes.

Their path was clearly lit.

And they were excited because they
had discovered the great light.

So it is . . . on certain cool, damp summer nights,
some may see the flicker of fireflies in the forest.

Still others may look into the night sky and see the
ever changing northern lights.

But a lucky few may catch a fleeting glimpse
of Aurora Mae and Borealis Burl.

# The Northern Lights

Aurora Borealis is the scientific name for the northern lights.
Although we see them at night, they are caused by the sun.

Because the sun is so hot, gases in it break up into free electrons
and protons. These are thrown out in a spiral shape as the sun rotates.
This stream of particles is called the solar wind.

When the solar wind strikes Earth's atmosphere, the collisions
of particle against particle give off energy in the form of colored
light—mostly green, but also red, blue, and violet.

That's when we see nature's gigantic light show in the sky.

# Fireflies

Fireflies, sometimes called lightning bugs, are neither flies nor bugs. They are a kind of beetle whose scientific name is pyractomena borealis.

A firefly's light is caused by a chemical reaction in its abdomen. The same chemicals are used to make glow sticks.

Fireflies seem to flash for three reasons. First, flashing is a good way to find each other. Second, fireflies taste bad, so predators learn that a flashing bug is not good to eat. And third, fireflies light up when they are in danger.

You might say they light up for another reason, too—to give delight to all who see them on dark summer nights. It's such fun to be out in a field or in the woods, see a tiny flash of light, and then wait and try to guess where it will next appear.

**Jeannine Anderson**, a special education teacher from Shoreview, Minnesota, has made a hobby of story telling. She has written several books for her four children and family. As a child, she watched the northern lights and, even then, felt the power and wonder in their beauty.

**Nikki Johnson**, a master painter with the Lake Superior Watercolor Society, paints the northern lights with skill and feeling. She has sold numerous paintings to galleries and collectors. She lives on the north shore of Lake Superior near Duluth, Minnesota.

**Joy Dey**, art director for a publisher for several years, is an award-winning book designer. She designed *Old Turtle* and *The Quiltmaker's Gift* among others. She lives with her family on a wooded estate north of Duluth, Minnesota.